A VAMPIRE'S WELCOME

"Gooooooooooood evennnning!"

I look down. There is a small bat, one of the smallest bats I have ever seen, standing at the bottom of the glass door. He has opened the door for me from the inside, and now is extending an open wing. "Why don't you *come in?*" he asks.

If I don't go in, there may be no way to rescue Grandpa Bat. I carefully step inside.

"Gooooooooooood," says the bat, in a voice far too deep for his size.

The door closes behind me and the bat flies up quickly to lock it shut. The bat seems larger in the dark.

"Do you have a friend here? Or business perhaps?"

"Y—yes," I answer. "I'm looking for a friend. His name is Grandpa Bat."

The bat shrieks in laughter, a sound so evil and strange that I want to run and hide.

"He is your friend?" says the bat. "That is too bad. Too bad for you!"

Other Bantam Skylark Books you will enjoy
Ask your bookseller for the books you have missed

BORN DIFFERENT by Frederick Drimmer

FIREBRAT by Nancy Willard

THE GHOST CHILDREN by Eve Bunting

GHOST TRAIN (Choose Your Own Adventure #120)
  by Louise Munro Foley

THE GLOVE OF DARTH VADER (Star Wars #1) by
  Paul Davids and Hollace Davids

LIZARD MUSIC by D. Manus Pinkwater

THE LOST CITY OF THE JEDI (Star Wars #2) by
  Paul Davids and Hollace Davids

WINGMAN by Daniel Pinkwater

THE WORLDWIDE DESSERT CONTEST by Dan
  Elish

ZORBA THE HUTT'S REVENGE (Star Wars #3) by
  Paul Davids and Hollace Davids

THE
VAMPIRE
STATE
BUILDING

by
Byron Preiss

Illustrated by
Kenneth R. Smith

Originally published as *The Bat Family*

A BANTAM SKYLARK BOOK
NEW YORK · TORONTO · LONDON · SYDNEY · AUCKLAND

RL 4, 008–012

THE VAMPIRE STATE BUILDING

A Bantam Skylark Book / published by arrangement with Byron Preiss Visual Publications, Inc.

PRINTING HISTORY
Originally published as The Bat Family
Caedmon edition published 1984
Bantam edition / October 1992

Book design by Alex Jay

ISBN 0-553-15998-4

Published simultaneously in the United States and Canada

Bantam Books are published by Bantam Books, a division of Bantam Doubleday Dell Publishing Group, Inc. Its trademark, consisting of the words "Bantam Books" and the portrayal of a rooster, is Registered in U.S. Patent and Trademark Office and in other countries. Marca Registrada. Bantam Books, 666 Fifth Avenue, New York, New York 10103.

PRINTED IN THE UNITED STATES OF AMERICA

CWO 0 9 8 7 6 5 4 3 2 1

Contents

Prologue

Winter · 1
The Crying Computer

Spring · 17
On the Links

Summer · 33
Blue Bear's Birthday Party

Fall · 53
The Vampire State Building

Epilogue

This book is dedicated to the cousins:
Dr. Joan Gold, Beth Preiss, Jeff Preiss
and Cliff Preiss, with love. —B.P.

For Angela, with love. —K.S.

Prologue

You know my house. It's a big house with lots of rooms. It has a big back lawn and another in the front with a long gate that faces the street.

My house has six tall pillars in the front and a balcony on the second floor. There are twenty-four windows in the front of my house and my room has a window that looks out on the front lawn toward the street.

It's white, my house, and in the snow you might not know it was there except for all the lights on inside and all the people who come and go. There are always people around my house whom I never get to meet. They come to see my dad. He's always busy, but then, so am I.

I have lots of friends that my dad never gets to meet. It's not that he wouldn't like to meet my friends, or that he wouldn't be friendly to them. He would. It's just that my dad is too busy to spend a lot of time with anybody now. He's very important. My friends understand, and so do I. My dad will meet them when he has the time and I'll meet his friends, too.

Maybe in four years...

WINTER

THE CRYING
COMPUTER

The Crying Computer

"No television!" said the man.

I wasn't very happy. Ever since my dad moved to the White House, people have been telling me what to do:

"No television!"

"No cookies!"

"No rockets!"

Everybody has a reason, too. "You can't watch television! People will think the President's kid can't read!"

"You can't eat too many cookies! The people will think the President's kid eats junk food all the time!"

"You can't have that toy! The people will think the President favors war!"

I try to tell them that I'm *not* the President, but they

don't care. "You always have to think of your father," they say.

I guess that's true. Some people do seem to care a lot about what I say. I'm just glad my friends don't get that way. My friends aren't people. Do you want to know what I mean? Listen.

My friends and I are in the basement of the White House. It's cold down here during the day. It's winter outside, and the White House lawn is covered with snow.

Some of my friends sleep down here. They don't make any noise. They don't snore. But when the moon comes out, they all wake up...except the youngest. He is strange. He wears big glasses and he can't sleep upside down, which would be perfectly all right, for a person. But like the rest of his family, he happens to be a bat.

The Bat Family has been in the White House for quite a while, and their ancestors arrived in America long before that. The first American Bat Family had hung from the sails of the *Mayflower* itself!

I look at my friends, the Bat Family: Grandpa, Poppa, Momma, Ginger and Bat, who doesn't hang upside down.

Bat is up, reading as usual. In his talons is a copy of a book.

"It's a manual," he says. "A book about computers."

I don't like computers. You always have to learn a dozen things just to use them, and when you finally learn, you find out that you could have done most of the things you were going to do on the computer just as fast by doing them yourself.

"Computers are *dumb*," I say.

"They *are* dumb," agrees Bat, "but a smart person can make them very smart. A smart person can make a computer think. All you have to do is learn the language the computer speaks and then use it!"

I hear many languages every day upstairs in the White House, but that's *not* the kind of language Bat means.

He means a *computer* language. Their languages have names like BASIC and ASSEMBLER and FORTH. These languages are really directions to a computer. Their words turn on and off the thousands of electronic circuits inside a computer. When those circuits switch on and off correctly, the computer seems to work as if it were thinking by itself.

"I have a computer," I tell Bat.

His eyes grow larger than ever. "You do? Could I see it?"

"It's a very weird computer," I say.

"What do you mean?" Bat asks. "Does it break down a lot?"

"It cries," I explain. "It's a crying computer."

* * *

6

We went upstairs, Bat flying, me walking. I let Bat into my room and he uses his built-in, natural radar to fly right to the giant closet.

"You found it," I say. "The computer's in the closet so it won't annoy anybody."

"Why don't you just shut it off?" asked Bat.

"You can't just shut off something that's crying," I explain. "It would be a mean thing to do."

Bat nods and opens the door with his wing. "Let's see it," he says.

In the corner of my very big closet sits a small computer. It has a gray keyboard, and a gray screen and little gray keys. It's *all* gray except for one red switch on its side. Next to the computer's screen is a little set of lines. Behind them is the speaker and from it comes a terrible, scratchy sound, the sound of a computer crying.

"What languages does it understand?" says Bat.

"I don't know."

"We can't talk to the computer if we don't know one of its languages. Isn't there any way you can find out? If you don't, it will probably keep on crying."

I start looking around the closet. My closet is a wonderful place to hide things, especially if I never want to find them again.

"There must be a manual somewhere," says Bat.

I start to walk toward the other side of the closet when I hear him say, "*Wait!* What's that?"

I look in the other corner of the closet and see something move. I know I didn't leave anything *moving* in here!

"Who are you?" asks Bat to the moving object which just happens to look like a pillowcase.

"It's me," says the pillowcase, who just happens to sound like my friend Puffin, the bird, who just happens to pull the pillowcase off with her beak and say, "I was taking a nap. Am I in the way?"

"We're looking for a manual," I tell Puffin.

"Can I help?" Puffin asks eagerly. "What type of manual are you looking for?"

"We're looking for a manual about my computer."

"We're trying to get it to stop crying," says Bat.

"When birds cry, we coo," says Puffin. "Why don't you coo to the computer?"

"Cooing is a language of birds," I explain. "The computer won't understand it. We need to find a language that the computer understands. That's why we're looking for a manual. It might tell us what to say."

I look on the closet shelves. There are plenty of comic books, and *Choose Your Own Adventure* books and even a couple of cookbooks, but I don't see any computer books.

"Think," says Bat. "Don't you remember reading the manual?"

"I read the first page once," I say, "but that was a long time ago."

"I think the crying sound is nice," says Puffin. "It helped me fall asleep. Maybe the computer is really cooing. How do you know it's crying if you don't speak its language?"

"I can tell crying from cooing," I explain.

"Do you remember where you left the manual when you read it?" Bat asks.

"I think I left it under the computer."

Bat reaches under the computer and pokes around with his wing. "There's a book under here. Maybe the manual got caught when you put the computer in the closet."

"Maybe." I put my hand under the computer and pull out the book. There's a picture of my computer on the cover.

Puffin chirps with delight. "You found the manual. Now we can find out how to talk to the computer."

"Open the book!" directs Bat.

I open it. On the first page is a message in English that I've seen before. It says, "A GIFT TO THE PEOPLE OF THE UNITED STATES FROM THE PEOPLE OF DENMARK."

"That's nice," says Puffin. "They gave the manual and the computer to America as a special gift."

I turn the page.

"Well?" asks Bat.

I turn another page. The entire book is in Danish. I

can't understand a word of it! The computer still is crying.

"You have a problem," says Bat. "You can't speak to the computer unless you talk its language, and you can't learn its language until you can read the manual. But there must be a way to stop it from crying."

I start looking around the closet for a Danish dictionary, when Puffin says, "Agatha! You should ask Agatha!"

That's a good idea. Agatha is smarter than anybody in the White House except my dad and Grandpa Bat, and she might be the smartest anteater in the world.

Agatha lives in a shed by the garden when it's cold. I put on my winter jacket and go outside with Bat and Puffin.

"Agatha!" shivers Puffin, knocking on the door of the shed. "Open up, we need your help!"

The garden is a good place for an anteater to live in winter. All the bugs go inside and the shed smells of grass.

Agatha slowly opens the door. "What do you want?" she asks. "I've only been asleep for a few weeks. You're not supposed to bother me until spring!"

"We can't stop a computer from crying—" whispers Puffin.

"A computer from *what*?"

"From crying," I say. "It's in my closet."

"Computers don't cry!" says Agatha.

I explained the story.

"Very well," says Agatha, "I will come look. Just let me put something on my snout. It's too cold outside to be walking around with my snout in the ground uncovered."

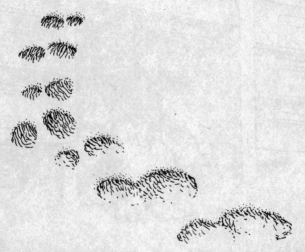

The computer was still crying when we returned.

"Isn't it sad?" asks Bat.

"Can you help it?" says Puffin.

"I don't know a lot about computers," Agatha observes, "but it's a horrible noise. She must be a very sad computer."

Just then, I hear footsteps outside my room.

"What's that?"

I recognize the voice. It belongs to a man from the Secret Service, the people who protect my dad and me.

"What's that noise?" he says, knocking on my door.

I hide Puffin and Agatha under my desk and Bat scurries under my bed, but the door to my room still opens before I can close the closet.

14

"What's that noise?" the man says to me. "It's coming from inside your closet!"

I hear Agatha gasp as the man pulls open my closet door.

"Static!" he shouts, listening to the computer's cries. "That static is almost deafening! Why haven't you shut this computer off?"

The man hits the red button on the side of my computer, and the crying stops. Then the man looks at me and smiles. "That was easy, wasn't it? It's a nice computer you have there. You shouldn't hide it in a closet. Do you know what language it understands?"

"Danish," I say.

SPRING

ON THE LINKS

On the Links

"Today," says Poppa Bat, "we are going to learn to play golf."

"Golf?" I ask.

"The game of champions! The sport of princes!"

"Why do they call it golf?" I ask.

Poppa Bat doesn't answer. He flaps his grand, gray wings and a little white, round ball, like a tiny snowball, plops down from them onto my bedroom floor.

I pick it up. "It's smaller than a football," I say. "I guess you don't kick it."

"Good," says Ginger, diving into my room through the window. "Guess again."

"It's smaller than a baseball," I say. "I guess you don't hit it with a bat."

"You're close . . ." Ginger suggests.

"But not close enough," says Poppa.

"Well, if you don't hit it with a bat, maybe you hit it with something else?"

My bedroom door flies open.

"*Ta-da!*" Blue Bear is standing just outside the door, waving a metal stick as long as my legs.

"This is a golf club," he explains. "You're going to love it."

He tosses it to me. It has a funny-looking silvery handle on one end, too flat to be the top of a cane. On the other end it has what seems to be a yard of dark-blue tape, all wrapped very tightly in a space no taller than my hands.

"Which side do I hold?" I ask.

Ginger flies down and wraps her claws around the tape. "This side goes into your hands," she says. "It's called a *grip*. You use the flat part to hit the ball. It's called the *head*."

This is all starting to make sense, but I'm not sure I'm interested. After all, what fun would it be hitting this little white ball with the little silver flat part at the end of a stick? Chances are that I would miss most of the time, and Puffin would have a good laugh—or squawk—at my expense. But everybody in the room is so excited that I feel obliged to find out more.

I pick up the ball and look at it. "It's not finished," I

say. The ball has little dents in its covering, all equal in size. "They haven't filled it in yet."

"The ball is finished," says Poppa Bat. "Those dents catch the air and make the ball fly better when it's hit."

"Well," I say, looking around my room, "there's only so far the ball can go if I hit it in here, and I don't think Dad would be very happy if I did."

"Look out the window," says Ginger.

I look down and see brightly colored poles all across the White House lawn. At the top of each pole is a little flag, each with its own number. At the bottom of each pole is a little hole. It really looks quite special.

"Golf," says Poppa Bat, "you're going to love it."

Well, the first thing I learn is that the funny stick with the tape and the flat silver head is one stick among many. There are actually six sticks that are the minimum I need to play golf nicely. There is someone to carry these golf clubs—he is called a caddy. The caddy gives a person the right club to use and is responsible for the ball after it's hit. "That way I get to lose the balls," says my caddy, Blue Bear. It sounds like a lot more fun than hitting them.

The second thing I learn is that in golf, unlike in football or baseball, there's nobody to catch what you're hitting except the grass, and the grass really doesn't care whether it catches your ball or not. Of course, I may be unfair to the grass. It's just that nobody's ever gotten an answer from the grass when they ask, "Why is it when a ball comes down you don't play catch?"

"*I* don't think the grass cares," says Ginger. "That's why it lets the dirt or the sand catch the ball so often."

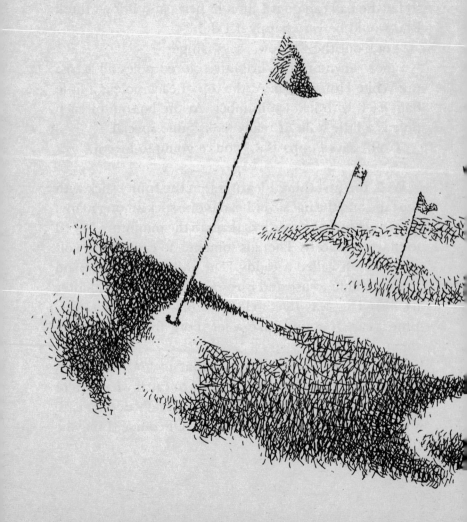

The third thing I learn about golf is that you *do not talk*. In baseball, everybody yells, including the umpire, who is supposed to tell you what to do.

In football, you have to yell or nobody hears you through their helmets.

Golf is a very quiet sport.

"The only time you talk," explains Poppa Bat, "is when you want to tell somebody else what to do. For example, if the person you are playing with is hitting the ball badly, you may tell him how to hit better."

"But won't that help him win?" I ask.

"No," says Poppa Bat, "it will just make you feel good. The person you tell will probably keep doing the same thing he was doing before you told him what to do."

"Then how do you win?"

"Winning is not important," says Blue Bear. "Agatha taught us that!"

"It may not be important," I say, "but I'd like to know how you do it."

"You win by getting the least number of hits to finish the game," says Ginger.

Golf is a very strange sport indeed! You have to hit a very small ball with a very funny-looking club and you're not supposed to talk about it unless you're trying to help somebody who probably wouldn't let you help them, and you win by not hitting the ball too much to nobody at all.

"Something is missing," I say. "You have to hit the ball somewhere!"

I found out as soon as I started to play. What was missing were the *holes*. The most important thing in golf is something that isn't there!

"You must get the ball in the holes to win," says Poppa

Bat. "If you don't get the ball in the holes under each of the eighteen poles, then you can't finish the game. Are you ready to play now?"

I nod. I have a feeling that the longer I play, the less ready I'll be.

"Before you make the first hit of any game," says Poppa, "you put this in the ground." He holds up a little wooden spike. "It's called a *tee*," he explains.

I take the tee and put it in the lawn, finding a little brown patch of soil that will support it without hurting the grass.

Blue Bear puts the golf ball atop the tee.

"Practice swinging before you hit the ball," says Poppa Bat. He shows me how.

I take the club and hold it in my hands, tucking one thumb under the palm of the hand that's lower down the club.

"Swing it," says Ginger.

I do.

"Good," says Poppa Bat. "Now approach the ball."

"I'm ready to caddy," says Blue Bear, holding a bag with five other clubs in it.

"I'll watch for the ball, too!" says Ginger.

I line up the wooden head of this golf club with the

ball, swing back and—miss! The ball is knocked off the tee by the breeze from my club.

"Too fast!" says Poppa Bat.

"Too hard!" says Blue Bear.

"Too high!" says Ginger, landing on my club.

I put the ball back on the tee, swinging slower, softer and lower and—miss!

"Too slow!" says Poppa.

"Too soft!" says Blue Bear.

"Too low!" says Ginger.

I try again, swinging faster, harder and higher. This time the ball is hit! It flies in a low arc across the lawn, but far away from the pole and the hole into which the ball is supposed to go.

"Good!" exclaims Poppa. "You hit it!"

We all follow Blue Bear, the caddy, to the place the ball has gone. It is now sitting directly under a tree.

"What do I do now?" I ask.

"As your caddy, I suggest you use another club," says Blue Bear. "You need something that will get you out of the thick grass under the tree. May I suggest this?"

He hands me a club with a metal head which has the number 5 on it.

"It's a five-iron," says Blue Bear.

"Don't swing it too hard," says Poppa Bat.

I swing and miss, again and again!

"It's all right," says Poppa. "Everybody does that the first time they play."

I'm getting tired of missing the ball. I look at the lawn ahead of me. The pole isn't too far away. If I don't hit the ball too hard, I might get close to it.

I swing the club back, look at the ball and hit it!

This time, though, the ball goes too far, sailing over the pole and down a little hill.

"Let's go find it!" says Blue Bear.

We all march to the hill, except Ginger, who flies ahead and spots the ball resting in an uneven circle of sand.

"A sand trap!" says Blue Bear. "This could be trouble. How about this?"

He hands me another club with a metal head. It has the number 9 on it.

"It's a *nine-iron*," explains Ginger. "It's good for sending the ball high in the air. It will help you get the ball out of the sand trap!"

I take the iron, swing back and hit the sand. The sand screams! I jump back and see a head peek out from the sand trap. It's Agatha!

"Since when does anybody bother me in my secret spot?" she asks angrily. "Don't you know manners when somebody is sleeping?"

"I'm sorry," I say, but Agatha keeps talking.

"Are you playing golf? Don't you know that golf takes

a lot of practice? You have to practice for hours and hours!"

"He's practicing by playing," says Poppa Bat. "I'm sorry if he bothered you."

"Hrumph!" says Agatha, and she digs herself back into the sand.

On the next swing, I hit the ball right toward the pole. Then I hit it closer, then farther, then closer, then farther, then closer, then farther, then closer, then farther, then closer, then farther, then a little closer, then a little farther, then even a little farther, then even a little closer to and from the cup.

"It's starting to get darker out," observes Ginger, about an hour later, while I'm still trying to sink the ball in the cup. "Maybe you should practice a little more."

I swing again and the little white golf ball rolls past the hole into which it is supposed to go again.

I look up and see my caddy Blue Bear. He is taking a nap against the tree. Poppa Bat is hanging peacefully asleep from the same tree, but Ginger still hovers overhead. I am very glad the little golf ball is white, because it is so dark out that it is getting hard to see. I am starting to think about dinner. First, though, I must finish this hole.

I take my club, which is now a *putter* with a flat metal head, and put it up to the ball. Then very slowly I aim

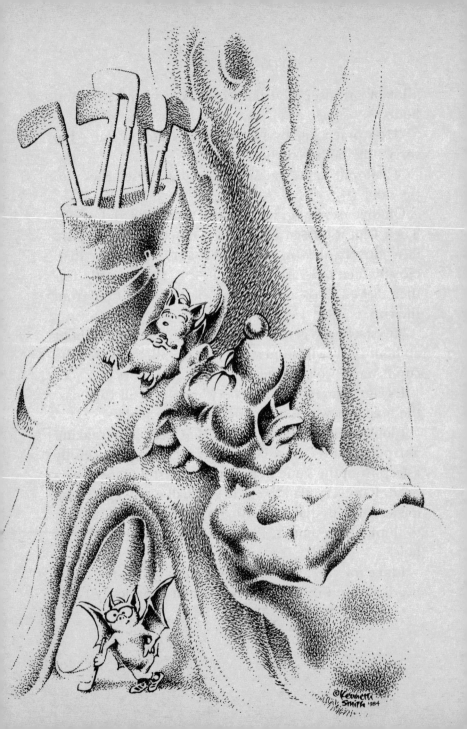

the side of the head of the putter at the hole and put it up to the ball. I swing back very softly and hit the ball. It rolls right into the cup.

"Hurray!" cheers Ginger.

Her shriek awakens Blue Bear and Poppa.

"He did it!" says Poppa.

"You did it! You shot a 78!" says Blue Bear. "That is the best score ever on this golf course! Only the best golfers get a score as low as a 78. You should be proud."

"Don't they shoot a 78 for the entire *game*, Blue Bear? I played only one hole."

"Don't worry," says Ginger. "It's a good start."

"It's still the best score ever on this golf course," says Poppa Bat.

"Yes," smiles Blue Bear, "it's the best score ever!"

I take my ball out of the cup and thank them all. I know I'm the first and only player to play this golf course, so my score has to be the best. Still I'm very happy playing on this golf course. My friends set it up just for me.

SUMMER

BLUE BEAR'S
BIRTHDAY
PARTY

Blue Bear's Birthday Party

"Does everybody have birthdays?" I ask Blue Bear, who is licking the chocolate covering off an ice-cream pop.

"Nope," he replies. "Don't you know?"

I wait for him to finish the chocolate part and start on the vanilla before I say, "Know what?"

"Such as I don't have a birthday," says Blue Bear.

"You have to have a birthday!" I protest.

"Well, I don't!" he says, and he sticks the entire vanilla part of the pop into his mouth and pulls it off.

"Agatha has a birthday," I reply. "She was born on the first day of May."

Blue Bear is not looking at me. We are sitting against

the stump of an old tree on the lawn which, unlike most tree stumps, is slowly growing.

"Grandpa Bat and Bobcat have the *same* birthday," I continue. "Remember the birthday party we gave for them, with melons and bubble gum and tea?"

"Nobody ever gave me a birthday party," says Blue Bear. He kicks his feet up and down a little, as if paddling in water on his back. "I'd *like* to have a birthday," he says.

"Didn't your Mom and Dad ever throw you a birthday party when you were growing up?"

"Nope." Blue Bear takes the stick from his pop and breaks it in half. "I never had a birthday party at all. No party hats, no little horns, no blue candles and no cake. No cake at all!"

I had never seen Blue Bear so upset. "Do you know why they never gave you a party?"

"They said I had too many brothers and sisters and if *I* had a party, then all my brothers and sisters should have parties, too! There wasn't enough food for that many parties."

"That seems fair," I say. "Your parents just wanted to have enough food."

"Well, it's easy for you to say. You always have birthday parties with lots of cake and ice cream and cookies and— oh, I'm making myself so hungry!" Blue Bear sticks half of the ice-cream stick back into his mouth.

"How come you never had a birthday party here?" I ask. "Everybody else has a party. Even Grandpa Bat who needs more candles than we can fit on a cake, has a party."

"I have a *problem*," explains Blue Bear. "I can't have a birthday party unless I know *when* my birthday is!"

I shake my head. "I don't understand."

"Don't you know what a birthday is?" says Blue Bear. He tries to stand, but his stomach is in the way. I give him a push. Blue Bear stands and turns around to face me, his arms open wide. "A birthday is the day you are born," he explains. "Agatha was born on the first day of May and so every May first we celebrate when she was born. Grandpa Bat was born on June sixth and every June sixth he gets a party thrown by the Bat family. I can't have a party because I don't know when I was born!"

"Isn't there a way for us to find out?"

"I don't know," says Blue Bear. "Bears don't usually write down the dates. We're too busy eating."

"Can't you write to your Mom and Dad and ask them?"

"I don't think they know either!"

I stand up, but I'm confused. What do you do when a bear doesn't know his birthday?

I go to see Poppa Bat.

He is hanging from the top of a lawn chair, the kind

with woven plastic strips that pinch you between your legs when you're sitting on them in shorts.

Poppa Bat is sleeping, of course, because the sun is out, but I think this is an important enough matter to wake him.

"Poppa Bat," I say, "can I talk to you?"

Before his eyes open, his ears perk up—or are they perking down, since he is hanging upside down?—and his wings lightly flutter. Poppa's bat radar senses are working. His big, dark, glassy eyes open. "What do you want?" he asks.

"I need help with Blue Bear's problem."

"Which problem? He has so many!" Poppa Bat does not sound glad to have been awakened, and now the sun is glaring in his eyes.

"Blue Bear's never had a birthday party," I say quickly. "He doesn't know when he was born. What do you do when somebody doesn't know when his birthday is?"

Poppa Bat flaps his wings and looks at me. "Do what bats do," he replies.

"What's that?"

"Make up a birthday. It doesn't matter *when* somebody was born. What matters is that they were born and that somebody is happy about it. That's why we have birthday parties. We want to celebrate the fact that somebody is here!"

I smile. "Do you think I should pick the date for him?"

38

Poppa Bat nods. "You know how hard it is for Blue Bear to make a decision. Why don't you just tell him the date you have in mind?"

With those words, Poppa Bat closes his eyes, wraps his wings around himself and goes back to sleep.

I go up to my room. I don't want to pick a date for Blue Bear's birthday that is already taken by somebody else's birthday. I don't want to goof up. After all, how many times in my life would I get to pick a birthday? I look at the calendar.

It is the sixteenth of July. Next week is my Dad's birthday, and I think I might get the chance to see him if he is back from his trip. The week after that is Ginger's birthday. Then it would be the first week of August, and that is when Puffin's birthday party will be.

That leaves this week, but it is Wednesday already. It would take a few days to get any good party set up. If everybody hurries, we might be able to throw a party for Blue Bear on Saturday night.

I look at the calendar again. July nineteenth it will be!

Blue Bear is floating in a little pond he and Agatha had dug out on the edge of the lawn at the beginning of summer. He is singing a little song and eating marshmallows from a bag on his stomach:

Blue Bear's Birthday Party

Oh, bears love melon and honey and stuff,
Bananas and bagels and lemon fluff,
But if I had to pick two things for my middle:
Marshmallows from a bag and pancakes on the griddle!

"I have a surprise!" I say, holding my hands behind my back.

Blue Bear grins. "Pancakes?"

"A birthday!" I answer. "A birthday of your very own! I picked it myself."

"Really?" asks Blue Bear happily. He stands up in the pond. "Can I see it?"

I laugh. "You can't see your birthday. A birthday is a day of the year. It's July nineteenth, Blue Bear!"

"July nineteenth..." he repeats, "July nineteenth... today is July fifteen—"

"Sixteenth," I explain.

"Today is July *sixteenth*," he nods. "Then the nineteenth would be Friday!"

"*Saturday*," I explain. "Blue Bear, your birthday will be July nineteenth!"

"Wow!" Blue Bear throws his handful of marshmallows in the air. They come flying down like tiny cotton birds and land gently in the pond.

"Am I going to have a party?" asks Blue Bear.

I take my hands out from behind my back and hand him the first of the invitations I have written out myself:

You are invited to Blue Bear's first birthday party. It will take place on the lawn on Saturday night July 19th.

Blue Bear reads it slowly, and then reads it again. He looks worried.

"What's the matter?" I ask.

"I'm confused," says Blue Bear. "Will this be my *first* birthday? If it is, then I'll be only one year old! I'll be younger than anybody I know. Even Bobcat will be older than me."

"Don't be silly," I say. "It's your first birthday party, not your first birthday. You're—you're—"

I don't know what to say. I don't know how old Blue Bear is either!

* * *

Maybe Momma Bat has the answer. I go to see her in the basement. She's hanging from the thousands of phone wires that run along the ceiling. She's reading a book called *Midbat Crisis*. I don't know what that means, and so I ask her.

"It's all about what happens to bats when they get older and their children leave home. What do they do then?"

"Grandpa Bat came to live with you and Poppa Bat," I say.

"That's why I'm reading this book," she explains. "I don't want to do the same thing to Ginger or Bat when I get older and they have families of their own."

"You don't like having Grandpa Bat share the basement with you?"

"No, no," says Momma, "I love Grandpa Bat . . . I just don't want to do the same thing he did when I'm his age."

"How old are you?" I ask.

"Well!" shrugs Momma Bat. "That is rather private!"

"I'm sorry," I say, "I'm just having a problem with Blue Bear and I thought you might be able to help me."

"How would telling you my age help you?"

"Well, let's say one year you didn't celebrate your birthday. Would that make you one year less old?"

"I wish it could, but it doesn't work that way, dear. Your birthdays add up whether you want them to or not."

"What if you didn't have a birthday in the first place? How would you add them up?"

"Everybody has a birthday! Everybody starts adding them up starting with the first!"

I shake my head and say, "Not everybody. Not Blue Bear."

The mystery wasn't solved, but Momma Bat told me that she would be delighted to come to Blue Bear's party. I gave the invitations to everybody else, and they all are coming! Now all that's left to do is to make sure the food and the gifts are ready.

Bobcat will be bringing the marshmallows, three bags of Blue Bear's favorite kind.

The Bat Family will be bringing a book—the very first book that Blue Bear will own.

I am bringing the food, fresh from the house.

Agatha would only tell me that she was writing a letter, but she wouldn't tell me which one. My guess is a "B."

It is Friday afternoon, tomorrow is Saturday night! Yet I still don't know which of Blue Bear's birthdays it could possibly be! He has even made up a little song about the mystery:

Blue Bear's Birthday Party

Well, I guess I'm one year old like a cub,
As silly as it sounds and it sounds real dumb,
I'm not ten, twelve or even twenty,
But I'm not complaining . . . one year is plenty!

He also made up a song about the party:

Hibernation is not for me . . .
I'm still too young too sleep, sleep, sleep!
My party is something to celebrate . . .
Marshmallows and cookies
I just can't wait.

Saturday night arrives. I put out the cookies, and the milk, and the fruit, and Bobcat's gift of three bags of marshmallows next to the old tree stump on the lawn. Ginger and Bat have surprised me by bringing party hats and horns, which everybody is now using. The noise is terrible! But Blue Bear is happy.

It's a beautiful summer night, warm and clear.

Blue Bear is sitting on the edge of the tree stump, singing a song to Ginger.

Grandpa Bat is flying in circles overhead, chewing on a cookie. I'm waiting for Agatha, who's bringing the birthday cake from her hut along with her gift for Blue Bear.

"You know," says Blue Bear, "I remember when I first came here. I was a little bear cub and it was raining and there was a big thunderstorm and this tree was knocked down by lightning!" He pats the tree stump. "It was very scary."

Momma Bat remembers my problem and asks Blue Bear exactly how long ago he first came to live at the White House.

"I don't remember," says Blue Bear. "I was *very* young."

"You must remember something else," says Ginger.

"All I remember is the storm," says Blue Bear, putting some milk in a cup. "There was lightning and this tree on the lawn came tumbling down!"

"It would have to have been this tree," says Poppa Bat. "There aren't any other trees on this part of the lawn."

"It *was* this tree," says Grandpa Bat. "I know all about this house and that's the only tree to have been knocked down in this century."

"Well, then," says Poppa Bat, "if this is the tree, then maybe we can solve the mystery of Blue Bear's age after all!" He swoops down and clasps his claws on the edge of the stump. "You said you were very young when you came here, Blue Bear?"

Blue Bear nods and blows his horn in agreement.

"Then," says Poppa Bat, tapping the tree stump with his claw, "here's how we can solve the mystery! Every

tree trunk has rings on it that can tell us its age. Each ring stands for one year. We can look at the rings on this stump and figure out how many years ago Blue Bear arrived!"

"Let's add them," says Blue Bear.

"Each ring stands for one year," says Poppa Bat, clawing one odd-shaped ring, "and this special ring shows the year when the tree was hit by lightning. All we have to do is add up all the rings that were made after the special ring and we'll know how many years it's been since Blue Bear arrived."

It was a good idea. We all started adding the rings on the outside of the tree stump and soon we had an answer: Blue Bear was twenty-four years old! There were twenty-four rings made after the special ring which showed the storm that had happened when Blue Bear first arrived at our house.

"I still don't know my real birth*day*!" says Blue Bear. "I just know how many years ago it was."

"Surprise!" comes a voice. We all turn around.

It is Agatha! She is carrying a beautiful cake, all lit up with twenty-four candles and pink icing. "HAPPY BIRTHDAY BLUE BEAR!" she shouts.

We all sing *"Happy Birthday to You!"* Then Agatha takes out a beautiful giant letter "B" that she has painted with her snout on a piece of brown cotton cloth, and gives it to Blue Bear.

"It's beautiful," says Blue Bear.
"Read the other side," says Agatha.
Blue Bear turns the cloth over and reads:

*To the Bluest of Bears, without any cares, from
your Mother, my sweet, who loves to watch you eat.
On the occasion of your first birthday,
July twenty-first.*

"Puffin and I found it hidden in the basement," says Agatha. "You must have had it with you when you first arrived here, Blue Bear, but you were too young to remember."

Blue Bear holds the cloth to his face and rubs it against his fur. Then he starts to cry. "It's from my Mommy," he says.

"Happy Birthday!" we all sing again. "Happy Birthday at last!"

Blue Bear smiles and looks at the cotton cloth. "July twenty-first!" he grins. "My real birthday is July twenty-first! Today is only July nineteenth!"

"I was close in picking July nineteenth," I reply. "It wasn't bad for a guess." I already know what Blue Bear is thinking.

"Can we have *another* party?" he asks. "On July twenty-first? With cake and cookies and marshmallows and—"

"Blow out the candles!" says Grandpa. "And don't ask for anything more!"

We all start laughing; one birthday party was enough for any year, any year at all and at last.

FALL

THE VAMPIRE
STATE BUILDING

The Vampire State Building

Part 1

I smile at Grandpa Bat and say, "You can't scare me. There is no such place as the Vampire State Building."

We are all sitting on the south lawn of the house. I am in my tree, watching Bat soar in circles above the rest of us. Ginger, Momma and Poppa Bat hang sleepily from a branch below me. On the ground, Agatha is reading a book about Danish computers, while Blue Bear snoozes. Over on Blueberry Hill, Bobcat and Puffin are devouring the last of our picnic lunch. It is the first day of autumn and I am as happy as can be.

55

Grandpa Bat, on the other hand, is in a bad mood. "You just don't believe me," he complains. "You just don't believe that there's a place so big, so scary that not even the bravest bat in America would dare go inside it if he didn't have to! You don't believe me that there's a Vampire State Building in New York!"

I grin and shake my head. "You're just telling stories to make *me* ask questions," I say. "I know how much you like to answer them!"

Grandpa flaps a wing at me in disgust. "You think I'm an old bat with tales to tell, don't you?"

"No, I don't!" I reach out to stroke his furry wing, but Grandpa thrusts out his bat chin and lowers the lids of his eyes.

"I'm hurt, very hurt," he says, "and I'm afraid you've forced me to do something I never wished to do, just to prove to you my bravery and honesty!"

With these words, Grandpa gives a ferocious screech and soars toward the sun.

"Grandpa!" I shout, shielding my eyes to spot him, but he is lost in the light above.

Grandpa Bat is missing. I know it now, a day later. I felt it last night. I thought about it this morning. It is my fault that he disappeared and now I have to find him. It wasn't nice for me to tease Grandpa about his stories, and now I will have to make it up to him . . . but where has he gone?

I need information. Grandpa Bat is the smartest member of the Bat Family. Poppa Bat is brave and strong, Momma Bat is clever and full of good advice, Ginger is as swift and graceful as can be, and Bat is a fast learner, but Grandpa Bat is the oldest and smartest of all. He has a lot of memories and a lot of rules in his head, but most of all he is a scholar. Grandpa Bat has more facts in his head than any other bat in America. It's not like Grandpa Bat to be bothered by anybody else's words, especially somebody as young as I am. Yet, as a result of what I had said to him, Grandpa has vanished.

I must find out where he has gone. I take a bag of fresh fluffy marshmallows, the kind that can sit and melt on your tongue for hours, and go to see Blue Bear under my tree on the south lawn.

"Hungry?" I ask him. He looks as though he is napping, so I speak softly.

"No," he says.

Now, there is one thing that all my friends here know: *Blue Bear is always hungry.*

"I am on a diet," he explains. "Agatha told me I am getting too fat."

"Very well," I answer. I put a marshmallow in my

mouth as quickly as I can so that Blue Bear does not get hungrier than he always is by having to look at it.

"Grandpa Bat is missing!" I tell him, and then I reveal my story, all the while hiding the bag of marshmallows behind my back. "I'm worried," I say.

"Well," says Blue Bear, "a person can be missing for lots of reasons. Sometimes a person doesn't know his way around and gets lost. If that's why Grandpa is missing, there's nothing to worry about. He's smart. He'll just ask directions or look at a map to find out how to get home."

"But he's been gone since yesterday," I explain, "and Grandpa Bat knows his way around Washington better than anybody. He would have been home before morning."

"Then..." smiles Blue Bear, who by now is sniffing the air for the marshmallow scent, "maybe Grandpa Bat isn't lost. Maybe he *knows* where he is and doesn't want to come home. Maybe he wants to teach you a lesson for teasing him about his story."

"It's not like Grandpa to punish somebody by disappearing," I answer. "He wouldn't want to worry us."

"Well, there *must* be a reason why he's gone," says Blue Bear, looking around my side now to find the bag of marshmallows behind my back.

"I'm feeling a little weak from my diet," he says. "Perhaps if I have something to eat I will be able to figure out where Grandpa has gone. A little sweet thing, lighter than air, whiter than snow, would do!"

"I thought you were on a diet," I reply.

"I have not had any lunch!" says Blue Bear. "Certainly a little lunch is a fair thing, even for a person on a diet."

"Would you like a marshmallow?" I ask.

Blue Bear extends his hairy paw and spears one of the marshmallows with his claw. Then he tilts his head back, opens his mouth, smiles, and drops the marshmallow in.

"It's like eating a cloud!" he exclaims and I hear the thing go down.

"Don't you want to let it melt on your tongue?" I ask too late.

Blue Bear frowns. "Is it good that way?"

"It's the best way," I answer. "It's like eating a large pillow made of honey and sugar."

"Then perhaps I should have another," sighs Blue Bear, "for I was so eager to get back to solving Grandpa's disappearance that I swallowed that first marshmallow as quickly as I could!"

I hold out the bag again and Blue Bear again dips his paw inside.

"Ahh!" he says as he rests the marshmallow on his tongue. "This is wonderful. It makes me sad to think of how I wasted the first! I don't think I shall be able to help you at all now. I am overcome by my own foolishness!"

"No!" I say. "Would you feel better if you had another marshmallow?"

"Can I?" asks Blue Bear.

I hold out the bag and he takes a third marshmallow, putting it on his tongue.

"I feel better," he smiles. "I think I know what we must do now. We must find out where Grandpa Bat was going before he disappeared. Then we might have a clue as to where he's gone."

"Bat spends a lot of time with Grandpa," I reply. "Maybe Bat knows."

"Very good," nods Blue Bear. "Let's go down to the basement and talk to him!"

Bat is awake during the day, as usual. The television is on, and the picture is upside down. All the other members of the Bat Family watch it at night.

"Hello Bat," says Blue Bear.

Bat doesn't answer. He is too busy watching the news upside down.

"That's not polite," I tell Bat.

"Look!" he says. "That's it! Grandpa Bat wasn't exaggerating! Look!"

I look. On the screen is the biggest, tallest building I have ever seen. At the bottom is a name: *The Vampire*

State Building! Almost all the windows in the building are dark, many are cracked, and at the very top is a giant rod. It looks like an antenna. Right now it is pointing downward, but that's only because the picture is upside down.

Grandpa hadn't been telling me a story. There is a Vampire State Building and it is in New York!

I tell Bat all about his Grandpa.

He offers to go to New York with me. "We can fly there and rescue him!" he says. "I'm sure Grandpa went to the Vampire State Building. He's always talking about it around this time of year when the leaves start to fall. But Grandpa's never gone there. He must really be upset. It's a dangerous place."

"I think you better stay here in case he comes back," I explain. "I'll go to New York alone."

"How will you get there?" asks Blue Bear.

"I'll go the same way my Dad does," I explain. "He just left a couple of days ago to make a speech in New York. He took the train from Washington to Transylvania Station in New York."

"Transylvania Station?" asks Blue Bear. "Is that near the Vampire State Building?"

"I don't know," I answer, "but I can find out."

On my way to the train station, I knock on Agatha's door. "Do you have a map of New York?" I ask her.

"New York is a big place. What part of New York?"

"Transylvania Station."

"Stay away from there!" she says. "It's dangerous. It's right near the Vampire State Building. Grandpa Bat's been talking about that area. You'd better think about something else. Why don't you practice with your computer? You look troubled."

I didn't have time to tell Agatha the whole story of Grandpa Bat's disappearance. I had to get to New York.

Part 2

I arrive at the train station and look for help. I've had to sneak away from the house, which I don't like to do, but any other way meant I'd be followed by two men in navy blue suits, who couldn't help Grandpa Bat because all they'd want to do is bring me back home.

No, the only way to help Grandpa Bat is for me to get to New York and reach the Vampire State Building. I know I can walk there from Transylvania Station.

"Where is the train to New York?" I ask a man in a blue cap.

"Which train?"

"The train to New York," I say again.

"Which train?" he says again.

"The train to New York."

"*Which* train to New York?" he says finally.

"I don't know," I reply, "how many are there?"

He points toward a little rack on the station wall. "You'd better look at a schedule," he says.

I walk over to the wall. There's a little wooden rack with lots of boxes. In each box is a set of identical papers each with the name of a place on it: *Baltimore, Philadelphia, Trenton, Newark, New York.*

I take one of the booklets that says *New York* and open it.

Inside are thousands of numbers, and the words, "SCHEDULE TO NEW YORK." There are dozens of columns inside, all with different times of the day or night. I don't know which to look at first!

Well, one of the columns says LEAVE and one of the columns says ARRIVE. I guess I'm leaving, so I look at that column first. Above all the numbers is a box of letters which says:

M-F except H*
H   except W**
W   except H***
H-W****

All of the little stars and letters look nice, but I wonder what they mean.

M-F? Well, it's a long ride to New York, maybe they

want to tell different types of people what the best ride would be: Maybe **M** means MAD and **F** means FUNNY. All MAD and FUNNY people should take those trains **except H**. What does **H** mean? HAPPY? HEALTHY? I don't know. If **H** means HEALTHY then what does **W** mean? WEALTHY? I'll look at the schedule again to see if it makes sense.

MAD and **FUNNY** people except **HEALTHY** people should take certain trains. **HEALTHY** people except **WEALTHY** people should take other trains and **WEALTHY** people except **HEALTHY** people should take even different trains. Then **WEALTHY** people who were **HEALTHY** would be on one train and **HEALTHY** people who weren't **WEALTHY** would be on another. That means the only people riding together would be unhealthy rich people and healthy not rich people! Did that make sense?

I need help, because on top of all of those columns were others for **AM** and **PM**. I know those mean morning and evening, but how does everything else fit in and what do those nice **** mean?

I look around for help. There is a red bear, actually a reddish brown bear, looking right at me.

"You can help me?" asks the bear.

"Can you help me first?" I ask him.

The bear looks a lot like Blue Bear, except for the

color of his fur and an accent that sounds unlike anything I have ever heard.

"Where are you from?" I ask.

"Russia," says the bear. "I am Russian bear."

"You took a train here from Russia?"

"No," he answers, "I took a plane."

"Then what are you doing in a *train* station?"

"I took a plane long time ago. I live in Washington
now," says the Russian bear. He is looking nervously
around the station, as if watching to see if somebody is
watching him.

"Why did you want to come to Washington?" I ask.

"I didn't want to *come* here," says the bear. "I was asked
to leave Russia years ago."

"Why?"

The bear lowers his voice to a whisper and looks
around the station. "They didn't like me. I was a *dissident*
bear," he said. "I disagreed with Russian government."

I'm not sure what *dissident* means but the bear keeps
talking in a voice I can hardly hear or understand.

"I lived in Russia, but I asked to hear the music of
freedom."

"What kind of music is that?"

"Listen!" he says. "It is all around you, here in the
station. People saying whatever they want to say. That
is music of freedom! In Russia, such music was heard

only in home, in private, never in train station! Never in public!"

"What kind of music *did* they have in train stations?" I ask.

The bear covered his ears and spoke as if words were coming out, but I couldn't hear anything.

"Speak louder, please," I ask.

The bear continues to move his lips, but again no sounds come out.

"I can't hear you!" I say.

Suddenly the bear lowers his hands from his ears, looks nervously around and then speaks aloud again. "Now you know how the music of freedom sounded in Russia," he says.

"I couldn't hear anything!" I say.

"Exactly," he answers. "It was silent. People had things to say but were afraid to say them. Police may have been listening! So people did not talk **in public**. I talked in public and the police didn't like me. They called me *dissident* and asked me to leave Russia. Now, years later, the music of freedom is being heard in Russia at last. I am happy. I am going to New York to fly home to Russia. Can you help me with the schedule?"

"That's what I wanted *you* to do!" I say. "Maybe we can help each other with the schedule."

"I *think* I know how it works," says the Russian Bear.

"You just take all of the numbers from one column and add them together. That will give you the time that the train leaves for New York. Look:

$$8:20$$
$$+ 5:19$$
$$+ 3:40$$
$$= 16:79$$

The train leaves at 16:79!" The reddish brown bear proudly folds his arms together, throws out his legs in a little dance and shouts, "*Hey!*" Then he smiles.

"That's crazy!" I say. "There is no such time as 16:79!"

"There *is* in Russia!" he explains. "There are twenty-four hours in a day and the sixteenth hour is your *four o'clock* in the afternoon. The sixteenth hour equals the first twelve hours of the day plus four more hours! Now you must figure out what to do with the other seventy-nine minutes."

$$12 \text{ hours}$$
$$+ 4 \text{ hours}$$
$$16 \text{ hours}$$

"Well," I answer, "there are sixty minutes in an hour. Why don't we subtract sixty from seventy-nine and add another hour to four o'clock? That would make it *five o'clock* plus nineteen minutes: **5:19**."

79 minutes	4 o'clock
− 60 minutes	+ 1 extra o'clock
19 minutes	5 o'clock

I look at the schedule again. "But the time 5:19 is already on the schedule," I explain. "Why would you add up all the hours to get an hour that's already in the schedule?"

"Da," sighs the bear. "It's a good question, that's why I need help."

"Well," I say, "what time is it now?"

The bear looks at a giant clock in the middle of the station. "It is 17:16," he says, "or as you would call it, **5:16**."

"Then let's find out if there happens to be one train for New York leaving at **5:19**!"

"Good idea!"

I go back over to the man in the blue cap and he tells me that there *is* a train to New York at 5:19. It will be leaving on Track 9. He says we'd better hurry if we want to make it.

We do.

Part 3

I am sitting in a small compartment with the reddish brown Russian bear waiting for the train to arrive in New York. We still haven't figured out the train schedule, but I can worry about that after I rescue Grandpa Bat!

It's dark outside, and I can see the lights of little houses that border along the track. My friend is sleeping, his snoring sound is keeping me awake. I wonder what Blue Bear is doing now. I wonder if anybody is worried about me back home, especially the men in the dark suits who wouldn't like it if I was missing. Dad won't miss me because he's already in New York, but I don't want anybody else to worry about me the way I'm worried about Grandpa.

I know what I will do. After Russian Bear wakes up and we arrive in New York, I will ask him to call home and tell everybody that I'm in New York and that I'm all right. Then nobody will worry!

Part 4

We arrive in Transylvania Station in New York. It is dark outside. I wake up Russian Bear, and give him some quarters that I have brought from my bank at home. I walk him over to a telephone booth and explain my plan.

"Da!" he says, which I now know means "yes" in Russian. He takes the quarters and says, "I will be glad to help you. Tell me: do you know how to use these telephones? They only have buttons, no dial! In Russia, all telephones have dials. They are *much* nicer than your buttons and make a pleasant sound when they turn."

"Just press the buttons for the correct numbers," I explain. "It's the same as putting your fingers in the holes of the dial."

"What number do you want me to call?" he asks.

"202–555–4088," I reply.

Russian Bear gets a strange look on his face, as if he is playing with the phone number in his mind. "What are you thinking?" I ask.

"How do I add up all of your phone numbers?" he says. "Two plus zero plus two plus five plus five plus five plus four plus zero plus eight plus eight! Those are a lot of numbers to add up before I dial!"

This conversation is starting to sound familiar. "Don't *add* them!" I say. "All you have to do is *press* the numbers to make a call. Be sure to tell everybody not to worry!" I start to say goodbye. "Good luck in Russia!"

"Be careful!" says Russian Bear. "You never know when somebody is watching you or listening to you or following you or smelling you or taping you or trailing you or watching where you go!"

I thank Russian Bear and head off.

I'm going to the Vampire State Building at last!

Part 5

I am very near the Vampire State Building.

It is dark here and the streets of New York look nothing like our fine White House lawn. There are newspapers in the gutter, garbage on the sidewalks and strange odors in the street, but there are also beautiful buildings soaring in the air. Bright lights are everywhere. Even with the buildings closed, the streets look like they are filled with twinkling colored stars.

I hurry in the direction Bat told me. At every corner, there are dozens of things to look at, but it is dangerous for me to be out here alone.

I quickly continue toward the Vampire State Building, and just as quickly I start to pass it by. There is no way to see how big it is as I walk down the street until I look up. Then I see it towering over buildings that would have looked gigantic almost anywhere else.

It is enormous, bigger than three battleships, as tall as a thousand people standing on top of each other. Where inside it could Grandpa Bat be?

The building is dark. Not a single light is on and not a single window is open. There doesn't seem to be anything moving, but that makes me more worried. What if something or somebody is watching me, hiding, waiting?

I have to find out.

I push in a revolving door, but it does not work. I try a glass door, but it is closed, too.

In the moonlight, I look around the entrance. In the middle of the black marble wall is a button that says, "Ring to enter at your own risk."

I push the button and there is a whirring sound. The revolving door starts spinning around! It's moving too fast for me to duck in. I watch it and wait until it suddenly stops. There still is no light in the building, but in the shadows, I can see something moving inside.

I ring the bell again. There is a loud screech that makes me cover my ears to block out the sound. I look up and see the glass door opening by itself.

"Goooooooood evennnning!"

I look down. The door hasn't opened by itself. There is a small bat, one of the smallest bats I have ever seen, standing at the bottom of the glass door. He has opened the door for me from the inside, and now is extending an open wing. "Why don't you *come in?*" he asks.

If I don't go in, there may be no way to rescue Grandpa

Bat. I think of all of Agatha's words of wisdom to me and carefully step inside.

"*Goooooooood,*" says the bat, in a voice far too deep for his size.

The door closes behind me and the bat flies up quickly to lock it shut. The bat seems larger in the dark.

"Do you have a friend here? Or business perhaps?"

"Y—yes," I answer. "I'm looking for a friend."

"An old friend or a new friend?" asks the bat, wrapping his claws together.

"Old," I reply, "very old. His name is Grandpa Bat."

The bat shrieks in laughter, a sound so evil and strange that I want to run and hide.

"He is your friend?" says the bat, throwing back his head. "That is too bad. Too bad for you! **Ha ha ha ha ha ha ha ha!**"

I decide it is time to get away from this crazy bat! Up ahead, I can see a little light in front of two doors. I start running.

I hear the laughter of the bat behind me. He's letting me run.

"There's no place to hide," he shouts. "This is the Vampire State Building! Do you know what that means? Do you know where you are?"

The bat streaks toward me and blocks my way just as I reach the little light. It is above a pair of elevator doors.

"The Vampire State Building is where all vampire bats live!" he shrieks.

"V—v—vampire bats?"

The bat smiles. I can see its little teeth glistening in the pale yellow light. "I am a vampire bat!" he says. "Would you like to find out why?"

"No!" I cry and with that I reach up and slap the little vampire bat.

I think I surprised him because he went down without even trying to get up. Before he can recover, I hit the button in front of the elevator doors and dove in.

The elevator car is completely black. I don't mind. At least I am away from the bat. But where could I go? I now know that Grandpa Bat has been inside the building, and might still be, but what did the bat mean when it said, "That is too bad for you!"? I'm not sure I want to find out, but I must if I want to find Grandpa Bat.

Before the doors of the elevator had closed, I had seen numbers on the buttons inside. There were one hundred and four of them and some were within my reach.

I push the button with the number two on it and the elevator car starts moving. A minute later, I step out on the second floor.

This floor is different than the first. All I can see in the faint light from the light above the elevator is a long hallway, with glass doors lining both sides. Way down at

the end, facing me, is an open door with a light on the inside. I start running toward it.

"Who's there!" comes a shout like an owl.

I duck inside and see a bat, a very old bat, resting in the corner of the room, unable to fly. He is a little larger than the first vampire bat. "Who are you?" he asks me.

"I'm looking for Grandpa Bat!" I say. I notice that this bat doesn't have any teeth. I was safe for the moment.

"You're too late!" says the old bat.

"Too late?"

"Too late to help him! He's crossed the 88th floor. I know. I have word of it."

The 88th floor? I don't understand at all, but at least I now know Grandpa is still in the building. "What's the matter with the 88th floor?" I ask.

"You entered the Vampire State Building without knowing about the 88th floor?" says the old bat. "Who are you? Are you crazy?"

"Grandpa Bat is my friend.

"Tell me what happened to him," I shout. "Tell me now!"

"Yell at your elders and I'll get you bitten in the neck!" says the old bat. "Now apologize!"

"I'm sorry," I whisper.—"I just want to find Grandpa Bat."

The old bat yawns. "You'll be sorry, you'll see."

"Please tell me where he is."

The old bat flaps his wings lazily and gets up. He walks over to a window and hops up on a ledge. Then he looks outside.

"You see this building," he says, looking up toward the top, "it was once filled with people."

I nod.

"Now it belongs to us. Vampire bats. There is one of us on every floor, and on every floor we get bigger! I'm twice the size of the little bat you met in the lobby, and above me is a bat twice my size. You should see the creature on the tenth floor!"

I don't want to think about it.

"Your friend Grandpa Bat is a brave old bat, but crazy. He only wanted to see the top floor! Only a crazy bat would want to do that! Nobody's been above the 88th floor since we moved in, except the little monster you met in the lobby. He knows what's up there. He told me. The bats above the 88th floor are so big that they take up almost the entire floor and they're so heavy they can never fly. Not that *I* can fly these days either! Your Grandpa Bat will be crushed by a giant bat the minute he leaves the elevator!"

"Maybe he flew up through the stairs," I say. "Grandpa Bat is smart."

"Maybe *he* did," replies the bat, "but *you* can't." He stares at the part of me where wings might be if I were a bat.

"You won't try to find out what happened to him if you value your own life."

I tell him I will find Grandpa, but I don't know what I'm going to do! If what he says is true, then there may be bats in the Vampire State Building as big as the White House itself!

I leave the old bat and head for the stairs, not the elevator. The doors in this stairway are glass. When I get to each floor at least I'll be able to see what's there.

The sun is coming up outside now. I'm hungry and nervous, scared, but I'm going to find Grandpa Bat. It's my fault that he's here.

Part 6

The tenth floor is dark. I don't see any bats flying around, but if what the old bat told me is true, then there should be a huge bat lurking somewhere inside.

I open the stairwell door and step in. I hear the sound of something breathing, wheezing. It must be a giant bat.

I follow the sound.

It's coming from around a corner at the end of the hall. I tiptoe toward it and peek around the edge.

Lying on its stomach is a big bat, but it is hardly as

big as the old bat made me think it would be. Was he telling me the truth? Were there really giant bats in the Vampire State Building?

"Help me!" says the bat in a high screeching voice.

I walk up to her slowly. She is on her side now and she looks sick. As I get closer, I can see her fangs.

"I tried to help him," she says. "I was brave!"

"Help who?" I ask, standing at her side.

"Grandpa Bat."

"Grandpa Bat? You saw Grandpa Bat?"

"He was friendly," she says. "He was crazy to come here, but I tried to help him! When he started flying up the stairs toward the 88th floor, I flew after him. But I'm too big now and too heavy to do that kind of flying. I'm all out of breath! I should have stayed here and warned him better!"

"Then it's true what the old bat said?" I ask. "There are gigantic bats at the top of the Vampire State Building?"

"Bigger than you could ever imagine! Bigger and fatter and more gigantic than you ever want to see. I tried to get Grandpa Bat to come back down, but he wouldn't listen."

That was just like Grandpa Bat. Once he decided to do something it was very hard to talk him out of it, but at least Grandpa was smart. He had taken the stairs up, not the elevator.

"I'll be all right," says the tired bat, "but you must leave. This is not a safe place!"

I knew that already.

* * *

I walk quickly back to the elevator door and stand outside. I could take the stairs up again, but that could take hours. Grandpa Bat had already begun his trip to the top floor long ago. If I was going to help him I would

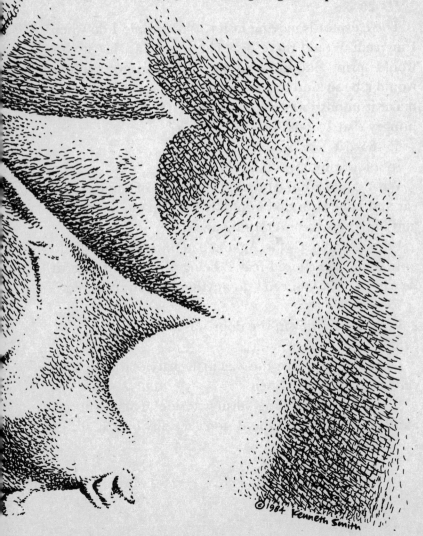

have to be there now. I had to risk the worst: I would have to risk having a gigantic bat coming out at me. I step into the elevator on the 10th floor. I push the button and speed toward the 88th floor.

15–20–25

The elevator is moving faster. What would I do when I arrived? Would there be a bat so *gigantic* that its fur would spring out and trap me in the elevator car? Or would it be so loud that the sound of its shrieking would make it impossible for me to hear? Or would it be so hungry that I would be a bat dinner?

55–65–70

In a few minutes, I'd be there.

What could I do? Hide in the corner of the elevator car and hope Grandpa would fly in? Run out screaming and hope to scare everything away?

I thought about what Agatha had once told me: "The only thing you should fear is being afraid. It is wise to be careful, but you can't do anything if you're scared."

75–80–85

I try to calm down; the door was about to open.

88!

I take a deep breath and wait in the back of the elevator car for the doors to open.

They do, but nothing springs inside! There's no gigantic bat waiting for me. I don't see any bats at all.

"Grandpa!" I shout, "Grandpa Bat!"

There's no answer.

I start walking down the corridor and then gasp. On both sides of me are windows with a view of New York unlike any other—a view in the sky! Grandpa Bat would love this view.

I shout again, "Grandpa Bat, where are you?"

I hear the sound of wings. Small wings. There is a familiar screeching sound. The vampire bat I had hit earlier is here . . . and he's angry!

I duck as he sweeps over me.

"How dare you hit me!" he says. "How dare you come up here! You should be frightened of the giant bats!"

"You're a liar!" I say. "There aren't any giant bats up here. It's a story! You made it up to keep the other bats away from the beautiful view! Now tell me where you hid Grandpa Bat!"

"*Hahahahahahahaha!*" shrieks the little bat. "You are a fool! Do you think vampire bats care about the view? Don't you know what kind of danger you are in right now?"

"You can't scare me," I answer. "Where are you hiding Grandpa Bat?"

Before he can reply, I feel the ceiling above us starting to shift. There is a loud thud, like something falling, like a foot falling, a giant foot.

85

"Now you will see who's a fool," hissed the bat. "Now you'll know what's happened to your friend!"

Before I can move, the ceiling starts to shudder and then crack. I dive for cover and the entire ceiling falls in! A giant foot breaks through! Then the furry brown body and wings of the most gigantic, fattest, hairiest bat on Earth appears—and in his claw *sleeps* Grandpa Bat!

"You have been looking for me?" says the gigantic bat.

I am too scared to speak, but I do. "I was looking for *him*!" I say, nodding at Grandpa Bat. "Is he all right?"

"He is hypnotized," says the gigantic bat. "We cannot let him escape. He can help me. I do not want to be in the Vampire State Building anymore, but I am too big to leave! I am too fat for the elevators, too big for the stairwells and too heavy for the floors! I have already fallen through from the 104th floor to the 88th floor and I haven't had a thing to eat since Tuesday. Maybe I'll eat *you*!"

With those words, Grandpa Bat awoke and saw me. "What are you doing here?" he asks. "Are you crazy?"

"I came to rescue you," I say. "Your life is in danger!"

"So is yours!" says Grandpa Bat. "This is all my fault. I just wanted to bring something back to prove to you that the Vampire State Building actually did exist. How foolish I've been. My pride has gotten us both in terrible trouble!"

The little bat slaps Grandpa Bat with its wing.

© 1964
Kenneth Smith

"Enough talking! You must help the giant. He is falling through floors faster and faster! If he keeps this up, he's going to ruin the whole Vampire State Building and himself!"

Grandpa Bat nods calmly. He doesn't show any fear, just like Agatha would have liked. "I have been thinking," he says. "There is one way out."

"Tell me!" says Giant Bat. "Or I will eat you."

"First you must let my friend leave," answers Grandpa.

"It's a trick," says the little bat.

"I don't care!" Giant Bat pushes me toward the elevator with his wing. "Get out of here!"

"No," I say. "I'm staying until Grandpa Bat is free."

"Go!" says Grandpa.

I don't move. There must be a way to help him.

"Tell me how to get out of here before I fall through another floor!" orders Giant Bat, ignoring me and the little bat.

"It's easy," says Grandpa. "You must fly."

"*Hahaha*," the little bat shrieks. "He cannot fly anymore. He is too big and too fat."

"No, he is not," says Grandpa Bat. "If his body has grown bigger, so have his wings. He can support more weight. Giant Bat must break through these windows and fly. They are the only windows in the building big enough to let him out!"

Giant Bat looks slowly out of the windows. "It is a very

big drop," he says. "If I'm not able to fly, I will be falling very far."

Grandpa Bat shook his head. "Fly or die," he says. "You know you can't keep falling through floors like this. Sooner or later you're going to hit something sharp!"

Giant Bat rolled his body toward the window. "Yes," he says, "there's nothing more I can do. I have to get out."

With that, the giant raises his heavy, fat and furry wings and smashes the thick glass. The wind blows in like a hurricane and he smashes the glass again.

"There," says Giant Bat, "it's all open, let's go!"

"Let's go?" I ask.

Giant Bat grins a mean smile. "If I go, you go. All of you, hang on!"

Grandpa Bat does not flinch, although the color in his brown face seems lighter. "Hold on tight," he tells me, "and keep your eyes open!"

Even the little bat seems frightened. "I think I'll fly down the stairs."

Giant Bat ignores him and sweeps Grandpa Bat and me up in his talon. This is it!

He leans forward and starts falling! I scramble onto his back before it's too late. Grandpa Bat is stuck in his claw.

"Oh no," groans the Giant Bat, "I've forgotten."

"Forgotten what?" I scream.

"How to fly!"

"Let go of me," says Grandpa Bat, "and I'll show you."

Here we are falling five floors at a time, and Grandpa is giving flying lessons to the biggest, fattest bat in the world!

"Now you try!" says Grandpa Bat.

"I'm nervous!" says the Giant Bat.

It is at this time that I notice all the other bats looking out of their windows at the Vampire State Building. The little bat must be screeching out the news as he descends the staircase inside.

"Flap!" says Grandpa. "Flap."

The giant starts flapping, and I feel us rise. Then we drop, then rise again. We are forty-five floors from the ground.

"I'm too heavy!" says the Giant Bat. "My wings are out of shape!"

"Flap!" demands Grandpa.

"It hurts!" whines the giant.

"Flap!"

We are twenty floors from the ground.

"There must be something else we can do," says the giant.

"Flap!" says Grandpa.

Eight floors to go. I can see the sidewalk as Grandpa hovers next to me.

"We're not going to make it!" says the giant.

I hold on tight to his fur. Then everything goes black.

The next thing I hear is Grandpa's voice and the sound of sirens. I know I'm alive!

"What happened?" I ask, standing up on the sidewalk outside the Vampire State Building.

"He bounced," says Grandpa Bat. "Giant Bat was so big and so fat that when he hit the ground, he bounced!"

"Is he all right?"

"He's unconscious, but seven ambulances are taking him to the hospital."

"Are *you* all right, Grandpa Bat?"

He smiles. "Well, I am angry at myself for being so stubborn. I insisted on proving to you that there was a Vampire State Building. I shouldn't have come here. I should have let you find out for yourself."

"I was stubborn, too," I answer. "I didn't take your word for it. I should have known that you wouldn't make up a story to scare me."

Grandpa Bat slaps my back with his wing. "It's quite an adventure we've had. I think everybody back home must be worried about us. Listen!"

A few seconds later, I hear what Grandpa's bat radar had picked up. A long black car, surrounded by two police cars, is racing in our direction.

"I'd better go," says Grandpa. "See you in Washington!"

Before the cars can arrive, he flaps off.

I recognize the men getting out of the car immediately. They're the men in the navy blue suits who are supposed to take care of me. They look very angry.

"We got a call from a Russian telling us that you were in New York!" says one of them. "We thought you had been kidnapped!"

"I'm fine," I answer. "I just had to find a friend."

"A friend? What sort of friends do you have here in New York? Your father will want to hear about this when you get back to his hotel."

Somehow, I don't think my Dad will believe it.

Epilogue

Well, one year has passed at the White House. I'm older now. I have more friends, too. Blue Bear's happy. He has his birthday. Momma and Poppa Bat are getting ready for vacation. They're going to see Yellowstone Park. Agatha and Bat are building a new computer and I'm going to learn how to use it. Puffin and Bobcat are waiting for snow so that they can make a snow mountain on the south lawn.

I'm looking forward to next Spring, when I can play golf again and when the south lawn will become a green carpet with little colored flags on poles. Then I'll take a bag of marshmallows outside and sing a little song that Blue Bear taught Grandpa Bat and me after we came home from New York:

> *Friends come in all colors*
> *Like blue and brown.*
> *Sometimes they smile.*
> *Sometimes they frown.*
> *It's not what they say,*
> *It's what they do*
> *That shows their love*
> *Is true to you.*

ABOUT THE AUTHOR

Byron Preiss is the co-author of *Dragonworld* (Bantam), the bestselling fantasy novel about which Maurice Sendak has said, "*Dragonworld* goes far beyond the flashy pyrotechnics of contemporary fantasy," and *The Little Blue Brontosaurus*. He is also the editor of *The Art of Leo and Diane Dillon*, a biography of the two-time Caldecott award–winning illustrators, and *The Art of Moebius*, a biography of the respected French fantasy illustrator. He works closely with the Bank Street College of Education on the Bank Street Ready-to-Read series for Bantam. He is a graduate of the University of Pennsylvania and Stanford University. Byron currently resides in New York City with his wife, Sandi Mendelson, a publicist, and his daughter, Karah.

ABOUT THE ILLUSTRATOR

Kenneth R. Smith is a respected illustrator, author, and professor of philosophy, which he has taught for many years at Louisiana State University. His most famous work is *Phantasmagoria*, a magnificently illustrated series of fables featuring lizards, fish, insects, and other fantastic characters. Portfolios of illustrations from these fables and other work by Mr. Smith have become treasured collector's items in recent years and are acknowledged masterworks of the fantastic. He has also illustrated *The Rebus Bears*, a Bank Street Ready-to-Read book (Bantam). He currently lives with his wife, Angela, and their children in Dallas, Texas.

Byron Preiss and **Kenneth R. Smith** have known each other for over twenty years. During this time, they have collaborated infrequently on books for young readers.